Goldilocks und die drei Bären

Goldilocks and the Three Bears

retold by Kate Clynes
illustrated by Louise Daykin

German translation by Nick Barkow

Goldilocks vergnügte sich damit, Blumen für ihre Mama zu pflücken.
Dabei geriet sie **tiefer** und **tiefer** in den Wald.

Halt Goldilocks, kehr um.
Auf jemanden, der ganz allein im Wald ist, lauern Gefahren.

Goldilocks was having fun, collecting flowers for her mum.
She was heading **deeper** and **deeper** into the woods.

Stop Goldilocks, go back home,
Woods aren't safe when you're all alone.

Sie entdeckte ein Häuschen mit einem schönen Garten.
“Die Blumen würde ich gerne pflücken,” sagte Goldilocks.
“Mal sehen ob jemand daheim ist.”

She found a cottage with a beautiful garden.
"I want to pick those flowers," said Goldilocks. "I'll see if anyone's home."

Halt Goldilocks, klopf' noch einmal.
Vielleicht lauert hinter der Tür etwas Fürchterliches.

Stop Goldilocks, knock once more,
There may be something grizzly behind the door.

“Hallo,” rief sie.
“Ist irgendjemand daheim?”
Niemand antwortete.

"Hello!" she called,
"is anybody home?"
But there was no reply.

Drinnen war ein Tisch mit drei Schüsseln. Eine grosse Schüssel, eine mittelgrosse Schüssel und eine kleine Schüssel. “Mmm, lecker, Porridge!” sagte Goldilocks, “Ich sterbe vor Hunger.”

On the table were three steaming bowls. One big bowl, one medium sized bowl and one small bowl. “Mmmm, porridge,” said Goldilocks, “I’m starving.”

Wach auf Goldilocks! Mach die Augen auf.
Sonst erlebst du noch eine grosse Überraschung!

Stop Goldilocks don’t be hasty,
Things could turn out very nasty.

Goldilocks nahm einen vollen Löffel aus der grossen Schüssel.
"Autsch!" schrie sie. Das war viel zu heiss.

Goldilocks took a spoonful from the big bowl.
"Ouch!" she cried. It was far too hot.

Dann nahm sie einen Löffel aus
der mittleren Schüssel.
"Uuch!" Das war viel zu kalt.

Then she tried the middle bowl.
"Yuk!" It was far too cold.

Das in der kleinen Schüssel war gerade
richtig - und Goldilocks ass alles auf.

The small bowl, however, was just
right and Goldilocks ate the lot!

Den Bauch angenehm vollgeschlagen, ging sie in das nächste Zimmer.

With a nice full tummy, she wandered into the next room.

Nun ist aber genug Goldilocks.
Du kannst nicht in anderer Leute Haus rumlaufen und alles angrabschen.

Hang on Goldilocks, you can't just roam,
And snoop around someone else's home.

Vor einem wärmenden Feuer standen drei Stühle.
Ein grosser Stuhl, ein mittelgrosser Stuhl und ein kleiner Stuhl.

In front of the warm, glowing fire were three chairs.
One big chair, one medium sized chair and one small chair.

Erst kletterte Goldilocks auf den grossen Stuhl, aber der war zu hart.
Dann kletterte sie auf den mittleren Stuhl, aber der war zu weich.
Der kleine Stuhl war gerade richtig.
Goldilocks lehnte sich zurück, da...

First Goldilocks climbed onto the big chair, but it
was just too hard.
Then she climbed onto the medium sized chair,
but it was just too soft.
The little chair, however, felt just right.
Goldilocks was leaning back, when...

...KNACKS! Die Beine brachen zusammen und sie fiel auf den Boden.
"Autsch," schrie sie. "Blöder Stuhl!"

Was hast du da angestellt Goldilocks?
Schnell steh' auf und lauf davon.

SNAP! The legs broke
and she fell onto the floor.
"Ouch," she cried.
"Stupid chair!"

Oh no Goldilocks, what have you done?
Get up quick, get up and run.

Goldilocks fühlte sich
sehr erschöpft und ging
die Treppe hinauf.
In dem Schlafzimmer
standen drei Betten.
Ein grosses Bett, ein
mittelgrosses Bett und
ein kleines Bett.

Goldilocks felt tired so she made her way upstairs.
In the bedroom were three beds.
One big bed, one medium sized bed and one small bed.

Sie kletterte in das grosse Bett, aber das war ihr zu gross und unbequem. Dann versuchte sie das mittelgrosse Bett, aber das war ihr zu weich. Das kleine Bett, das war gerade richtig, und bald war sie fest eingeschlafen.

She climbed up onto the big bed but it was too lumpy. Then she tried the medium sized bed, which was too springy. The small bed however, felt just right and soon she was fast asleep.

Wach auf, Goldilocks! Mach die Augen auf,
sonst erlebst du noch eine grosse Überraschung!

Wake up Goldilocks, open your eyes,
You could be in for a BIG surprise!

In diesem Augenblick kamen
die drei Bären heim. Nachdem
er über den Korb mit den Blumen
gestolpert war, entdeckte Vater Bär
den Esstisch.

Just then the three bears came home.
After tripping over a basket,
Father Bear noticed the table.

"Jemand hat meinen Porridge gegessen," rief er mit durchdringender Stimme.

"Jemand hat meinen Porridge gegessen," rief Mutter Bär mit halblauter Stimme.

"Someone's been eating my porridge," he said in a loud gruff voice.

"Someone's been eating my porridge," echoed Mother Bear in a medium voice.

"Jemand hat meinen Porridge gegessen," rief Baby Bär mit feinem Stimmchen, "und sie haben nichts übriggelassen!"

"Someone's been eating my porridge," cried Baby Bear in a small voice, "and they've eaten it all up!"

Drei sehr hungrige Bären fühlten ein leichtes Unbehagen,
aber konnte ein blumenpflückendes Monster sehr
furchterregend sein?

Three very hungry bears, feeling slightly wary,
But a flower-collecting monster
doesn't sound too scary.

Sie nahmen sich bei der Hand und schlichen sich ins Wohnzimmer.
"Jemand hat auf meinem Stuhl gesessen," sagte Vater Bär mit lauter, brummiger Stimme.
"Jemand hat auf meinem Stuhl gesessen," sagte Mutter Bär mit halblauter Stimme.

Holding hands, they crept into the living room.
"Someone's been sitting in my chair,"
said Father Bear in a loud gruff voice.
"Someone's been sitting in my chair,"
echoed Mother Bear in a medium voice.

"Jemand hat auf meinem Stühlchen gesessen," klang das Stimmchen von Baby Bär, "und sie haben es kaputt gemacht!"
Und fing an laut zu weinen.

"Someone's been sitting in my chair," cried Baby Bear in a small voice, "and look, they've broken it!"
He burst into tears.

Jetzt waren sie sehr besorgt.
Leise schlichen sie sich die
Treppen hinauf ins
Schlafzimmer.

Now they were very worried.
Quietly they tiptoed up the
stairs into the bedroom.

Drei angsterfüllte Bären, nicht ahnend
was sie vorfinden würden,
ein stuhlzerstörendes Monster der
übelsten Art?

Three grizzly bears, unsure
of what they'll find,
Some chair-breaking monster
of the meanest kind.

"Jemand hat in meinem Bett geschlafen," grollte Vater Bär mit tiefer Stimme.

"Someone's been sleeping in my bed," said Father Bear in a loud gruff voice.

"Jemand hat in meinem Bett geschlafen," rief Mutter Bär mit halblauter Stimme.

"Someone's been sleeping in my bed," echoed Mother Bear in a medium voice.

"Jemand hat in meinem Bett geschlafen,"
heulte Baby Bär, mit lauter Stimme.
"Und seht mal da!"

"Someone's been sleeping in my bed," wailed
Baby Bear in a far from small voice,
"and look!"

Der Lärm weckte Goldilocks auf und sie schrie.

The noise woke Goldilocks up and she screamed.

Während die Bären sich von ihrem Schreck erholten...

While the bears were recovering from their shock...

...sprang Goldilocks aus dem Bett, rannte die Treppen hinunter,
griff sich ihren leeren Korb und floh.

Goldilocks leapt out of bed, ran down the stairs,
grabbed her empty basket and fled.

Geschiet dir ganz recht, Goldilocks,
die Bären haben dir einen schönen
Schreck eingejagt.
Noch ein kleines Geheimnis, ganz unter uns:
Die drei Bären waren auch ganz schön erschrocken!

Well Goldilocks, it serves you right,
Those bears gave you a terrible fright.
But here's a secret that must be shared,
The three poor bears were just as scared!